SUPER DUCK

First published in hardback in Great Britain by HarperCollins Children's Books in 2008

10 9 8 7 6 5 4 3 2 1

ISBN-13: 978-0-00-727326-3

ISBN-10: 0-00-727326-6

HarperCollins Children's Books is a division of HarperCollins Publishers Ltd.

Text and illustrations copyright © Jez Alborough 2008

Visit our website at: www.harpercollinschildrensbooks.co.uk

Printed and bound in China

For Stuart

SUPER DUCK

Jez Alborough

HarperCollins *Children's Books*

Sheep and Frog are looking for Goat;
he's not in his house, he's not in his boat.

'I'm here in my shed,'
he cries with delight,

'look what I made…
a beautiful kite.

Come on you two, let's see if she'll fly.
Now who can throw my kite really high?'

'Me!' comes a quack, loud and clear.

He reaches out and grabs the kite   then hurls it up with all his might.

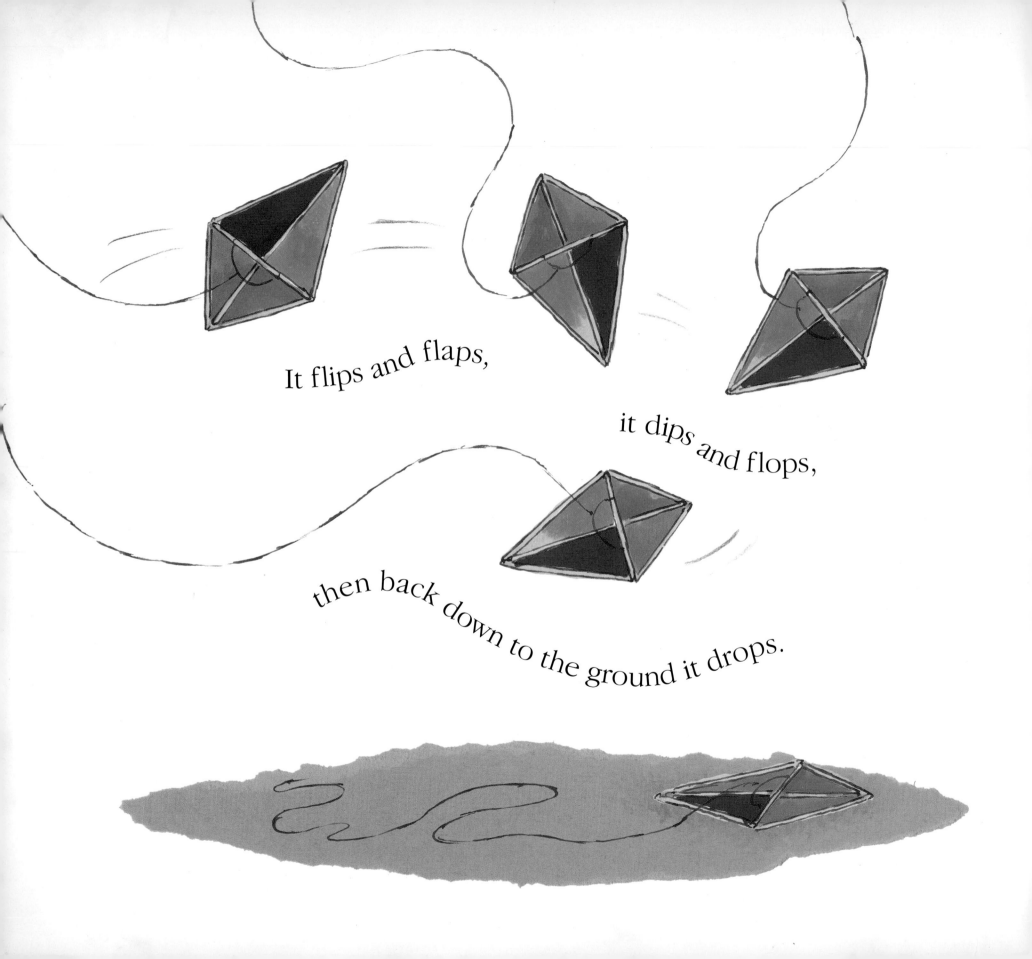

It flips and flaps,

it dips and flops,

then back down to the ground it drops.

'A kite,' says Goat, 'needs more than a fling,
someone has to pull the string. Someone strong must run and steer…

He grabs the string and shouts out, 'GO!'
then scampers off with kite in tow.

It flits and skits and flutters around
but refuses to rise very high off the ground.

'It needs to go faster,' thinks Super Duck.
'I know, I'll use my super fast truck.'

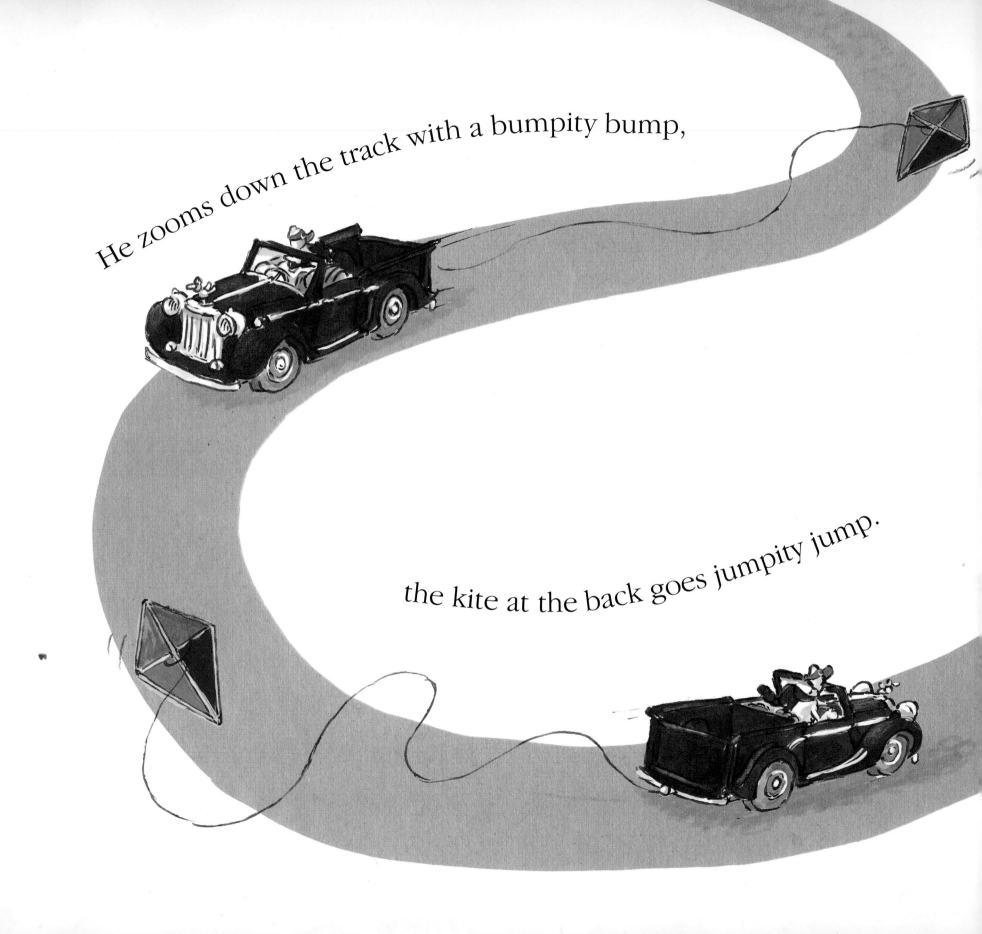

He zooms down the track with a bumpity bump,

the kite at the back goes jumpity jump.

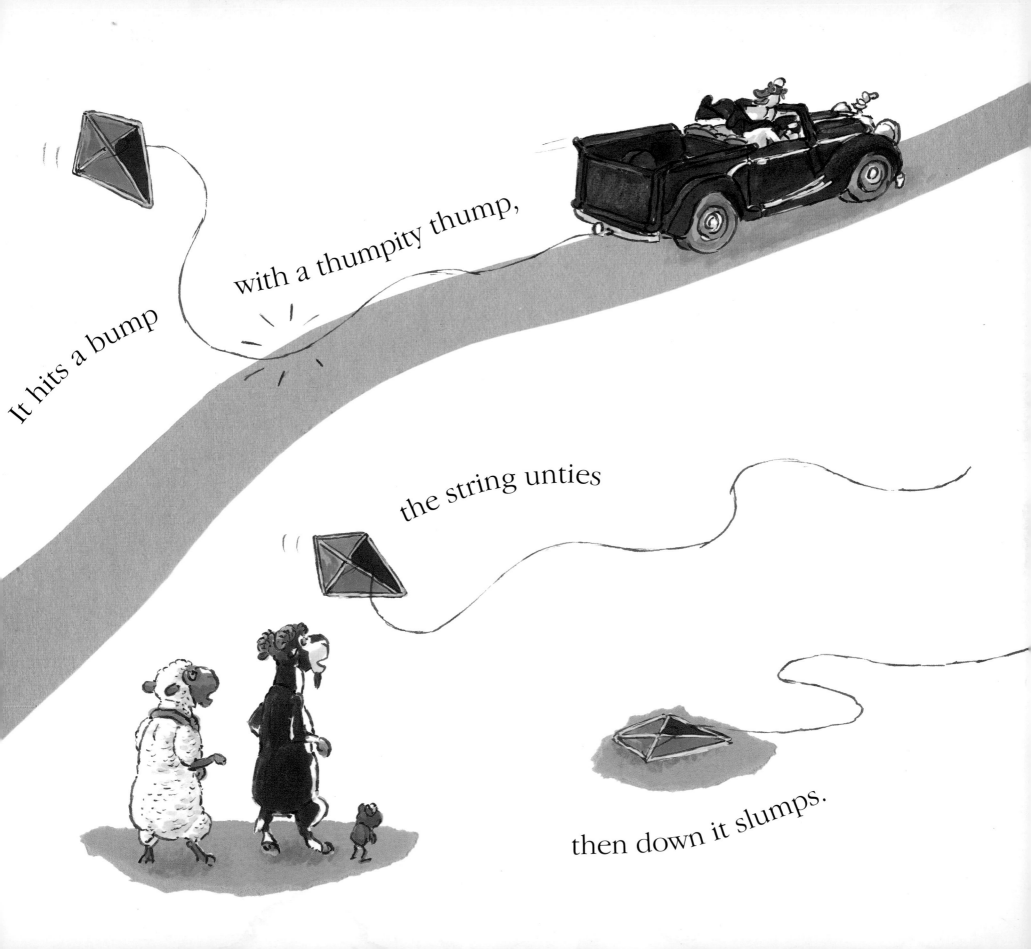

It hits a bump

with a thumpity thump,

the string unties

then down it slumps.

Goat says, 'No matter how hard you try,
without any wind the kite will not fly.'

Just at that moment
Goat's beard starts to twitch,

something blows up Sheep's nose
with a tickle and itch.

'It's the wind!' yells Sheep, 'it's come out to play,' as the kite takes flight,

and whooshes away.   'Help!' hollers Frog,   hanging on at the rear…

He jumps in the truck – brmm-brmm, beep-beep.
'Wait for us,' cries Goat. 'We can help,' yells Sheep.

'Grab the string,' quacks Duck to Goat in the back,
as the truck goes bumpity-bump down the track.

'The kite is too high,' yells Goat, 'it's no good.'
'Take the wheel!' yells Duck, as he climbs on the hood.

It shudders and judders but Duck doesn't care,

he teeters and totters,

then leaps in the air…

on to the string which swooshes and swings,

as he climbs his way up

with his super strong wings.

The kite begins to jiggle and thrash.
'The tree!' wails Frog. 'We're going to crash.'

'Jump!' shouts Duck as he lets go of the kite,

then with a *WHOOSH* the pair take flight.

Duck swoops

and he loops

and cries, 'Never fear...

Goat and Sheep call out, 'Where's Frog?'
'Oh dear,' says Duck, who is stuck in a bog.

'He should be on my super cloak.'
Then suddenly they hear a croak.

Goat looks up and starts to cheer,
Sheep wipes away a sheepish tear,

as shaken, stirred, but safe and sound, Frog floats gently to the ground.

'You saved me,' he cries

as he lands in the bog. PLOP

'I did,' says Duck, 'I saved my friend Frog.'

Then Goat and Sheep run into the muck…

shouting, 'You're a hero, **SUPER DUCK**!'